CALEB'S
FRIEND

for my friend Chris

Thanks to
Denis Serkin and James Carmichael

Library of Congress catalog card number: 92-54646
Published simultaneously in Canada by HarperCollins*Canada*Ltd
Printed and bound in the United States of America
by Berryville Graphics
Designed by Martha Rago
First edition, 1993

Eric Jon Nones

CALEB'S
FRIEND

Farrar, Straus & Giroux

New York

For as long as Caleb could remember, the sea was part of his life. First in his father's boat, learning all that he could about being a fisherman. Then, after his father died, working alongside the men from his village who made their lives on the sea as well.

Days on the boat were hard, but Caleb never complained. Each evening, he would take out the harmonica his father had taught him to play. Its comforting music filled the quiet night.

One day, the catch was especially good and everyone worked hard to bring it in. Later, when Caleb began to play his harmonica, it slipped from his tired hands and fell into the sea.

Caleb couldn't sleep; the night seemed empty. Instead, he sat staring at the moon and listening to the waves against the ship. Suddenly he saw a boy reach over the side and set the harmonica on the deck. Startled, Caleb jumped up. The boy looked him straight in the eye, smiled broadly, almost laughing, and then was gone. Caleb ran to the side, but the boy had vanished.

Caleb looked at his harmonica shining in the moonlight. "Maybe it didn't fall overboard. Maybe I was dreaming."

The following day Caleb sat alone, mending nets. He
heard a splash, and then another. He looked up but saw only
a tail fin among the waves.

"What kind of fish was that?" Caleb wondered aloud as a
crewman walked by.

"Who're you talkin' to, mate?"

"A fish, I guess," Caleb answered.

Just then, the boy from the night before popped up behind the crewman's back, waving his hands and splashing water on the deck. When the crewman turned to see what was happening, the boy disappeared.

The man went back to his work, and Caleb searched the water, mumbling, "He must be here someplace. He can't stay under forever."

No sooner had he said this than the boy burst out of the water, arched through the air, twisted, and dove back into the sea.

"No one is ever going to believe this!" Caleb shook his head in amazement. As the boat headed into port, Caleb never took his eyes off the water. But there was no sign of the boy.

The next day, Caleb walked for hours along the shore, thinking about the boy from the sea. Toward evening, he took out his harmonica and played, the notes floating across the water. Before the song ended, the boy was there.

"I thought I might not see you again," Caleb began. "I wanted to thank you." The boy didn't seem to understand his words, so Caleb clasped the harmonica in both hands and pressed it against his heart.

Then Caleb held out a wild summer rose, the only gift he could think to offer. "I brought this for you." The boy from the sea put it up to his face and smelled, for the first time, the perfume of a rose. A look of wonder crossed his face as he clutched the flower gently to his heart and slipped down beneath the water.

The next morning, while Caleb was working at the harbor, the boy from the sea suddenly appeared again and handed him a magnificent seashell. It was like no other shell he had ever seen. Before Caleb could thank him, his new friend winked and disappeared just as quickly as he had come.

A few days later, the mackerel were running off the coast and every fishing boat in the village raced out to catch them. The nets had to be spread and taken in, again and again.

All at once, the fishermen stopped working. They stared in disbelief at something caught in one of the nets. At the sudden silence, Caleb looked up as the men began to circle around the creature who was both boy and fish.

"Captain, what should we do with this thing?"
a crewman asked. "Throw it in the hold with the rest of
the fish?"

"No, you can't! You mustn't!" Caleb shouted. "He's just
a boy."

"That is no boy, Caleb. You can see that," the Captain said.

"Then let him go back where he came from."

"Let it go? Not while I'm on board," another man
argued. "There's money to be had here, and lots of it.
That's why we fish, to sell our catch. This will fetch a
high price, and I know just who will pay it." The others
nodded, and Caleb's pleas fell on deaf ears.

A day's sail up the coast, Caleb's friend was sold to a
merchant, who counted his money twice as he told them:
"Normally I don't buy freaks, but maybe some circus
sideshow will want it." The man smiled to himself,
knowing that he would make a fortune. Later, Caleb saw
people gathering at the warehouse, buying tickets from the
merchant. Through the doorway he could see the spectacle
inside.

As he watched the crowd gape at the boy from the sea, Caleb's shock turned to anger.

That evening, long after everyone had left, Caleb broke into the warehouse with an iron bar. It took all his strength to get his friend onto a rickety wheelbarrow. They raced to the harbor and the end of the dock, where the water was deep and safe. Caleb hugged his friend tight, then tipped him into the black water.

Caleb snuck back to the ship before anyone found out
what he had done. They set sail for home on the early tide.
Caleb kept to himself. "I hope he's far away by now."

During the night watch, the lookout warned of storm clouds blowing up fast from the southeast. A sudden gale began to drive the boat toward the coastline. The helmsman struggled to regain control of the ship, but in the darkness of the storm they could hear only the howling wind and the terrible sound of the waves crashing on the jagged rocks, which seemed to be all around them.

"Look!" someone shouted. "There, in the water."

Caleb's friend rose from the waves between the reef and the ship, motioning with his arms toward the open sea. Caleb was able to direct the helmsman until the boat was safely away from the rocky coast.

As the ship cleared the headland and sailed into deep
water, Caleb looked back from the stern, but he caught only
a glimpse of his friend in the distance.

When they returned home, Caleb was kept busy unloading the catch and repairing storm damage. As soon as the work was done, he rowed an old skiff out onto the sea, far from the shores of his village. The silver harmonica flashed between his hands. As the song finished, there, by the side of the skiff, was his friend.

They both laughed aloud, just from happiness. Caleb played another song while his friend swam around the boat as if he were dancing.

Finally, after hours had passed, they knew it was time to part. The boy in the water reached toward Caleb, pretending to take a rose and smell its fragrance.

Caleb's heart missed a beat. How could he explain that roses bloomed only for a short time and already they were gone? He thought a moment, then took his harmonica and placed it in the palm of one white hand, folding his friend's fingers closed around it. As he had so many weeks ago, the boy from the sea pressed the gift to his heart and quietly sank down into the water.

From then on, until he was a very old man, Caleb returned to the village every year. He would walk along the shore, listening, remembering. Then he would throw an armful of roses across the water and watch as they drifted out to sea.